Bunny and Bee's
Rainbow Colours

Sam Williams

For Rusty, Dusty, Kibble,
Rolo and Rex

Also available:

Bunny and Bee's Noisy Night

Bunny and Bee's Playful Day

Bunny and Bee's Forest Friends

ORCHARD BOOKS
96 Leonard Street, London EC2A 4XD
Hachette Children's Books
Level 17/207 Kent Street, Sydney NSW 2000
1 84362 185 1 (hardback
1 84362 610 1 (paperback)
First published in Great Britain in 2004
First paperback publication in 2005
Text and illustrations © Sam Williams 2004
The right of Sam Williams to be identified as the author
and illustrator of this work has been asserted by him in
accordance with the Copyright, Designs and Patents Act, 1988.
A CIP catalogue record for this book is available from the British Library.
1 2 3 4 5 6 7 8 9 10 (hardback)
1 2 3 4 5 6 7 8 9 10 (paperback)
Printed in Singapore

Here is a house.
A house in a tree.

The house is the home
of Bunny and Bee.

Bunny   Bee

Today they wake early
to wash and brush.

Then put on their boots
and outside they rush.

White fluffy clouds
float by in the sky.

Bee tries to touch them,
but they're much too high.

From the little seeds
that Bunny and Bee have sown,

plump orange pumpkins
are now fully grown.

"Round red berries
on a green holly tree,
remind me of Christmas,"
says Bunny to Bee.

Brown leaves flutter
down from the trees,
falling this way and that
in the autumn breeze.

Then Bunny and Bee
feel the rain, drip drop.

The sky turns grey,
and it rains, spit spot.

A rainbow shines
on Bunny and Bee.

It is time to go home
to their house in the tree.

Outside their home,
in the cold black night,
the big white moon
shines its light.

Inside their home,
all snug in their tree,

it is warm and cosy
for Bunny and Bee!